This book belongs to:

EVa

Dedicated to all my friends I've met along the way.

Books in the series...

Written by Katie Lorna McMillan
Illustrated by Graeme Andrew Clark
First printing 2019
ISBN 978-1-9997427-5-1
Published by Laughing Monkey Publishing

www.laughingmonkeypublishing.co.uk
email – info@laughingmonkeypublishing.co.uk

Find us on Facebook at
Haggis MacDougall – The mouse with a very long tail

For more illustrations by Graeme Andrew Clark,
visit - www.oldmangrey.com

Haggis MacDougall and the Dinosaur Egg

Written by Katie Lorna McMillan
Illustrated by Graeme Andrew Clark

To Eva
Merry Christmas!

My Name is Haggis MacDougall. I have a very long tail for a mouse.

It helps me on my adventures, every time I leave the house.

My tail used to drive me mad and left me feeling sad.

But now I think it is wonderful; it makes me really glad.

I stopped the ship at an island. It looked perfect to explore.

I jumped off the ship, into the sea and swam up to the shore.

The island looked like paradise; palm trees and golden sand.

I couldn't wait to see who I would meet in this new land.

The first friend I met was a little crab. Her name was Clawdia Snip.

She introduced herself, shook my paw, but she gave me a little nip.

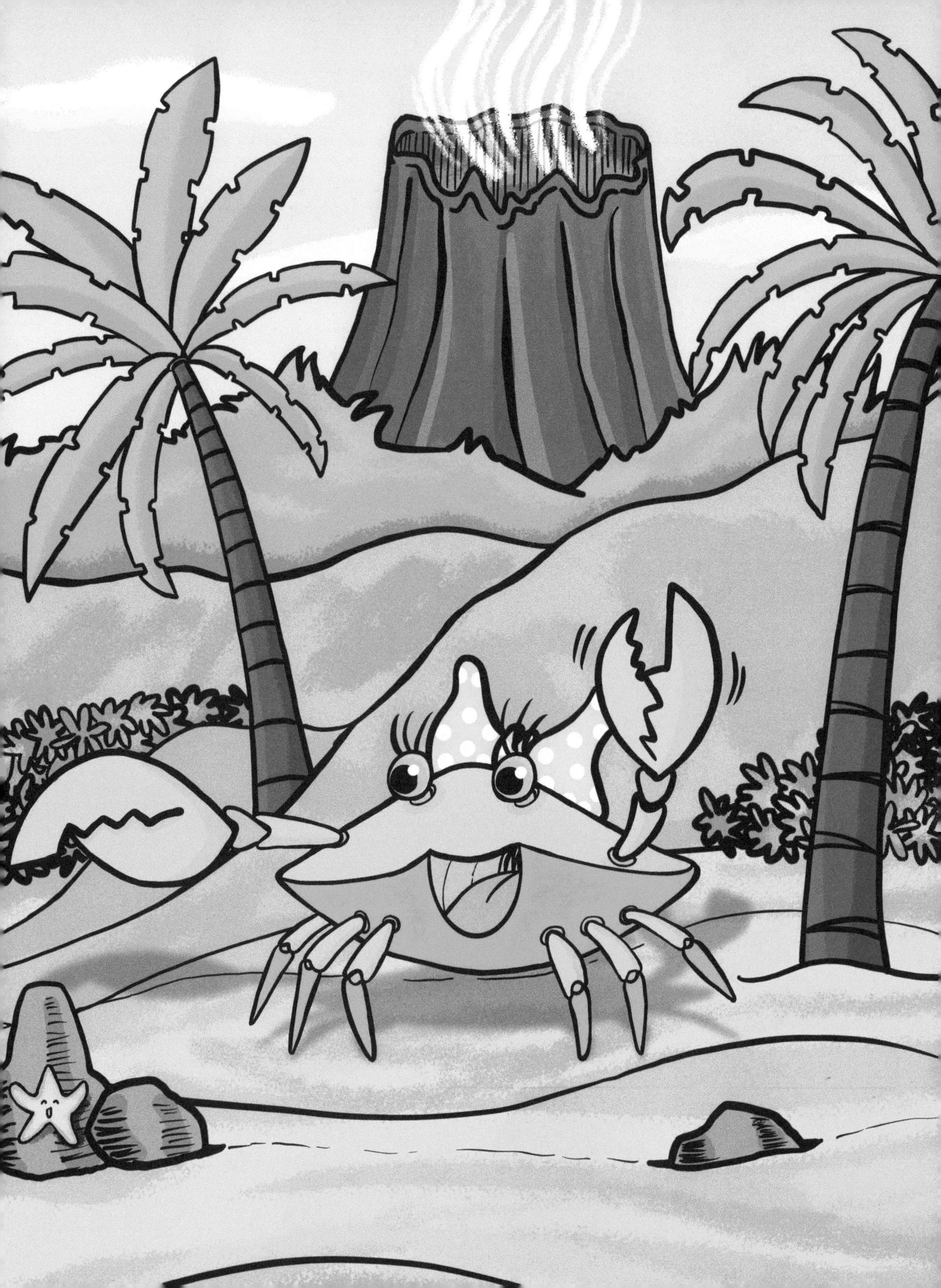

"Ouch!" I said, "Your claw is sharp, my paw is small you know.

You must be careful! Don't snip off my finger or my toe."

"Oh sorry," cried Clawdia, "I didn't mean to hurt you, little mouse.

I have a plaster for your paw in my seashell house."

Her house was over the sand dunes, under the biggest palm tree.

It was made from beautiful, shiny shells that she collected from the sea.

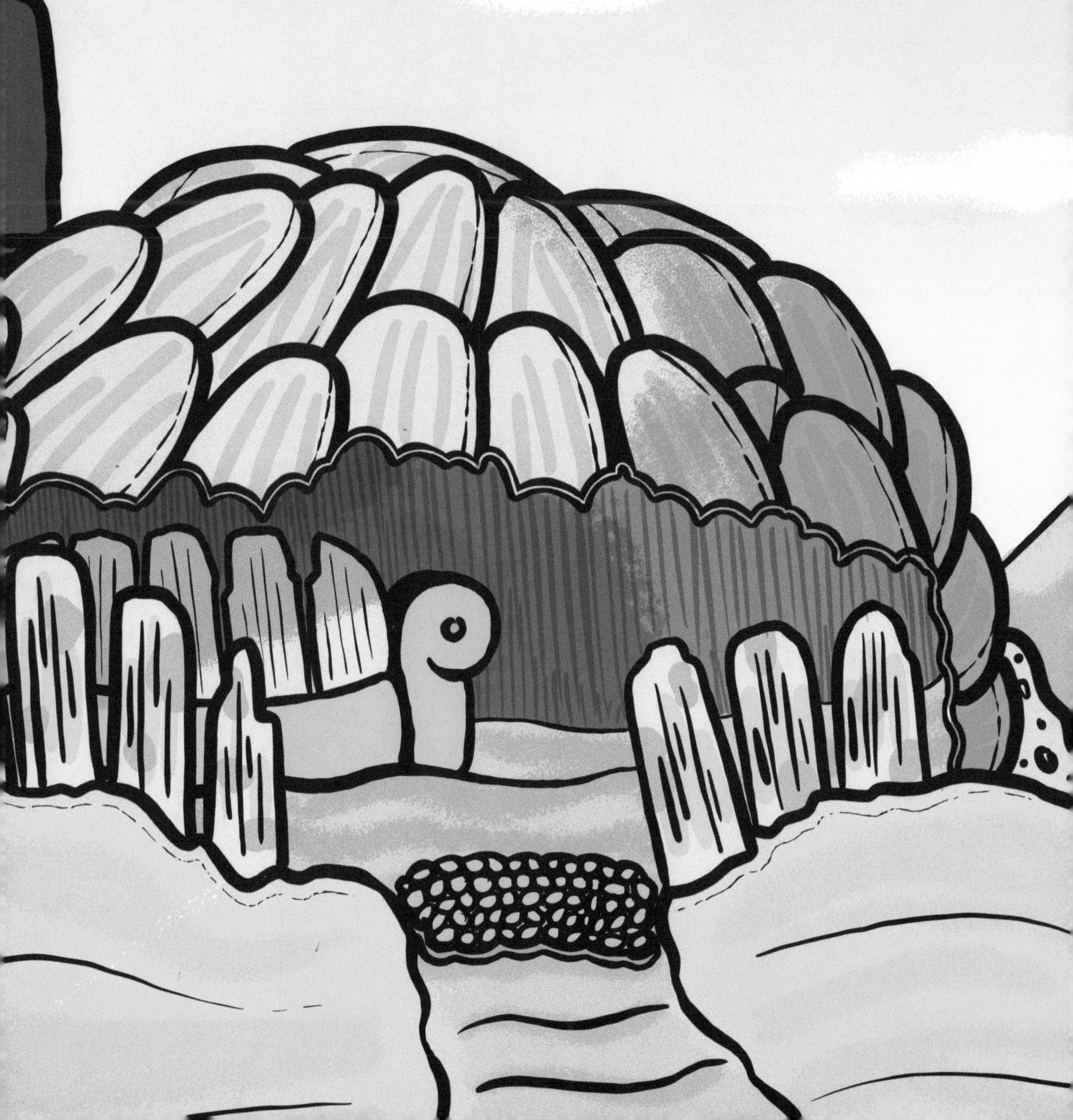

She placed the plaster on my paw,
then we set off to explore.

We found an old volcano
that didn't erupt anymore.

"Wow!" I said, "I've never seen a volcano this close before."

"Don't worry," said Clawdia, "it hasn't erupted since 1874."

We climbed a little bit closer, to have a look inside.

And that's the moment we found an EGG nestled into the side.

So I said to Clawdia...

"What is an egg doing down there and why is it all alone?

How will we get it out and safely back to its home?

It looks a little cracked, I hope the baby is okay.

Clawdia Snip, can you crawl down and check without delay?"

Clawdia sidestepped carefully until she arrived at the egg.

She could see it moving gently, and tapped it with her leg.

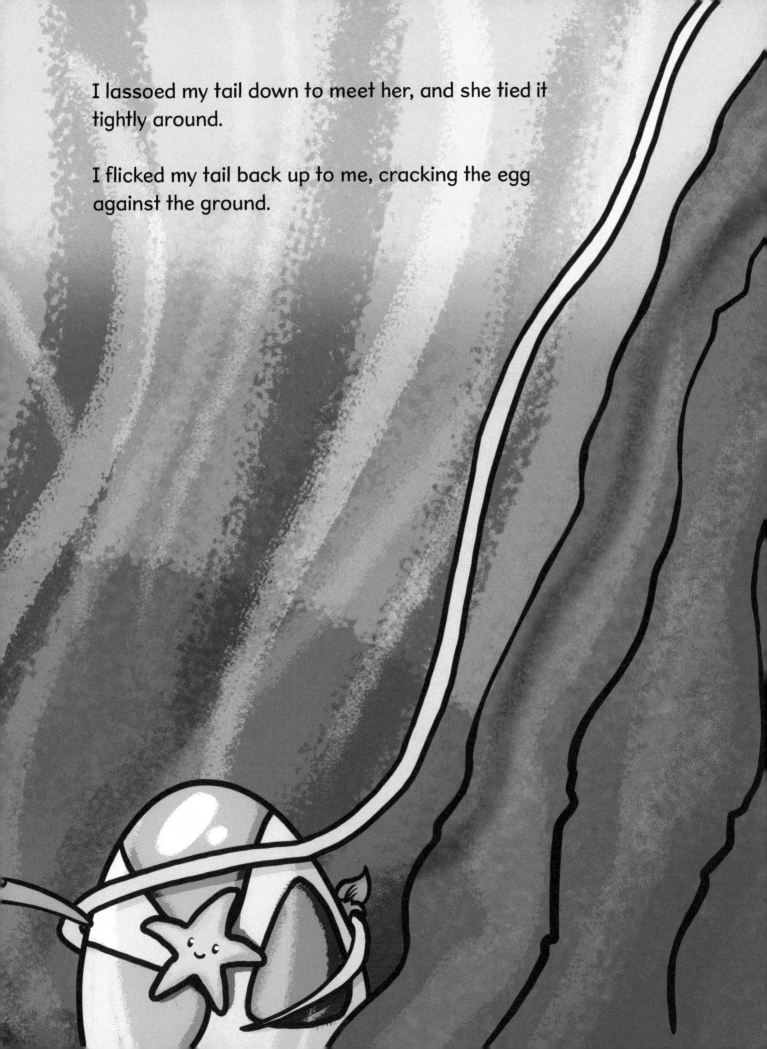

I lassoed my tail down to meet her, and she tied it tightly around.

I flicked my tail back up to me, cracking the egg against the ground.

CRACK!

We ran over to the giant egg
to take a closer peek.

It cracked and out popped four large baby feet.

It cracked again, out came a head
and it gave a roar!

You'll never guess what stood before us
- a diplodocus dinosaur!

The baby dinosaur roared, and we heard a rumbling sound.

We heard a distant roar, and there was shaking on the ground.

The baby dino was crying and it gave a louder ROAR.

All of a sudden I looked up to see THE MAMA DINOSAUR!

"ROAR. ROAR," roared Mama dinosaur, and she gave a little smile.

"Thank you for finding my baby egg, she has been lost for a while."

"My pleasure," I said, **"let me show you where the egg was found.**

We tied my tail around the egg, and brought it up to the ground."

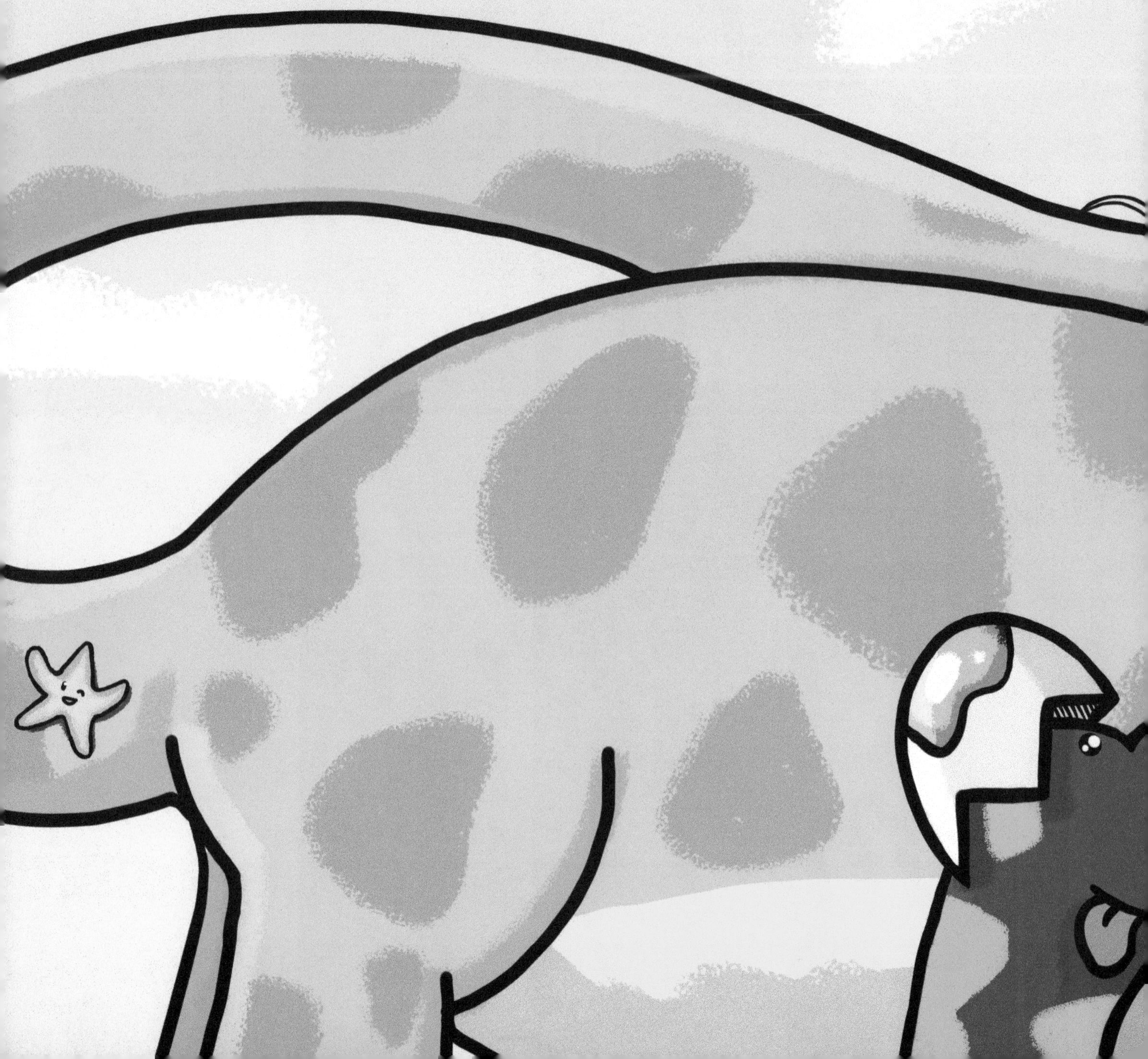

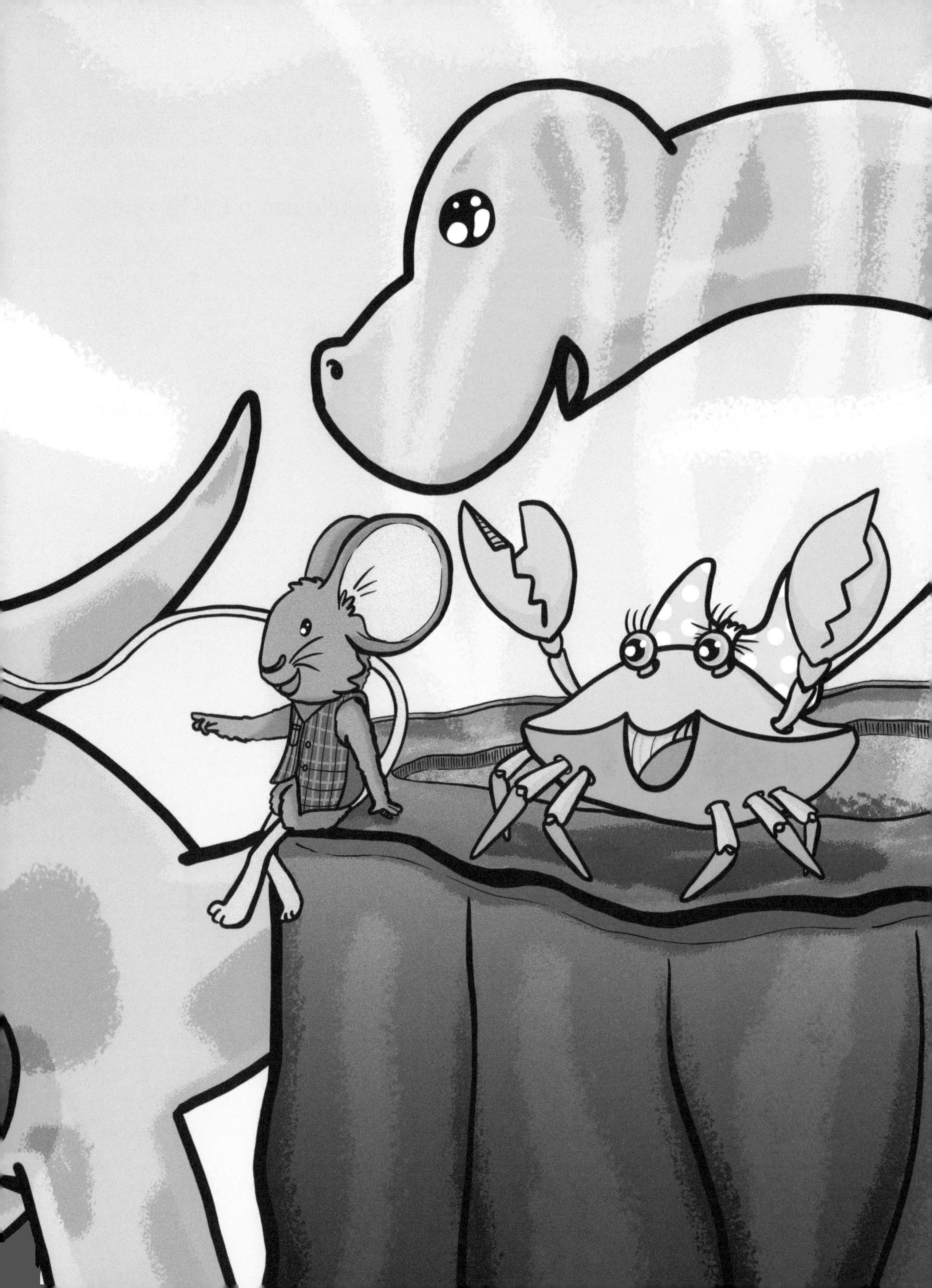

"Wow!" said Mama dino, "How useful your tail is!

Our baby eggs always roll around; we could use a tail like this."

The baby Dino thanked Clawdia too, and invited us for tea.

"Please come to see our home; it's just behind that tallest tree."

So we followed the dinosaurs to celebrate the rescue.

There was Tyrannosaurus rex, Triceratops and Stegosaurus too!

"This adventure has been great, I thought you were all extinct."

"Let's keep it our secret," said Mama dino, as she smiled and winked.

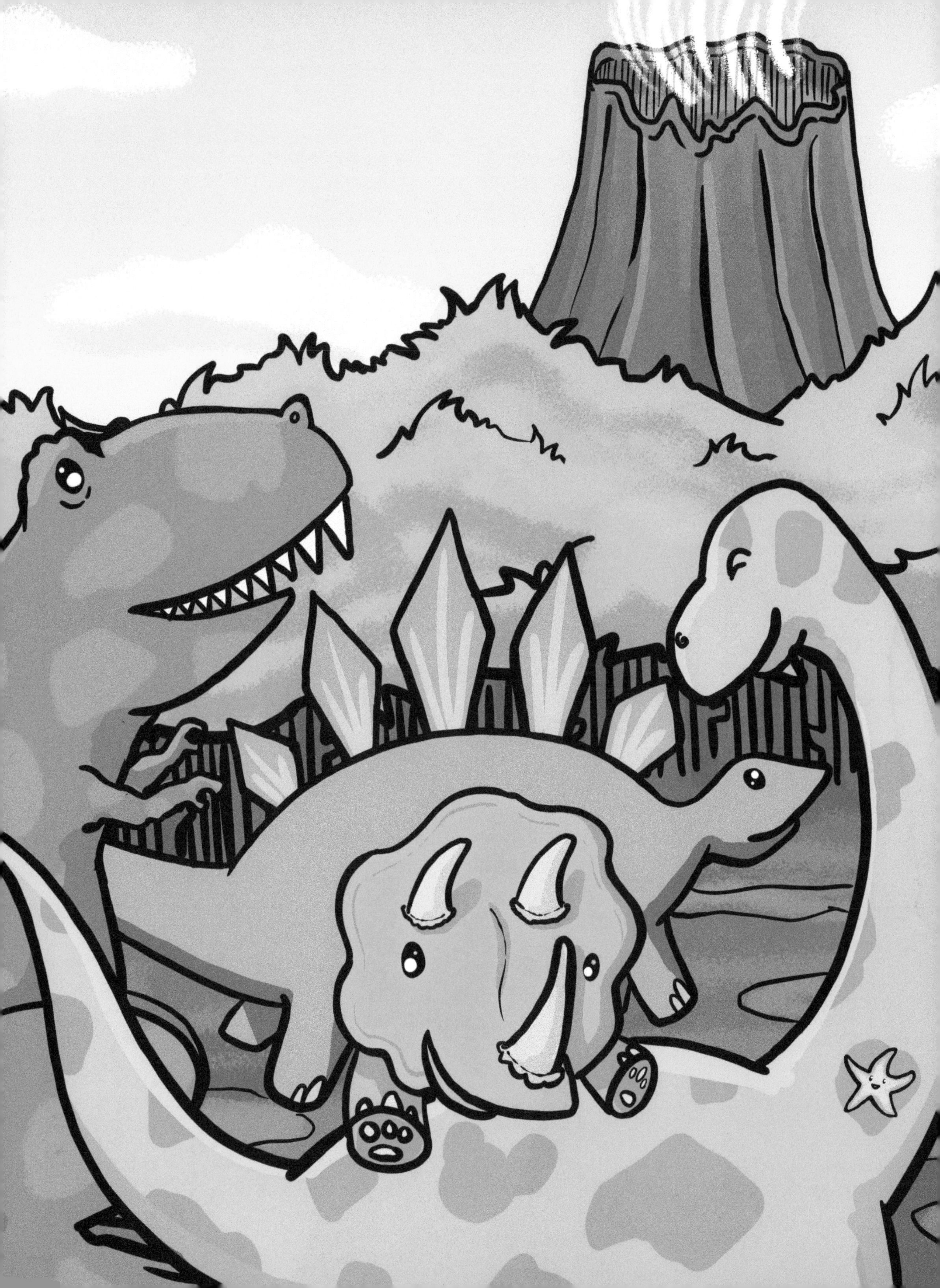

So that's the end of this story and Haggis is so proud of his tail.

He tried to rescue the dino egg and he certainly didn't fail.

It is great to make new friends in life,
and show them you really care.

So always smile, be helpful and kind,
and you'll always have friends there.

 # The Haggis Quiz

1. Who was the first friend Haggis met on the island?

2. Where does Clawdia Snip live?

3. What did they find in the volcano?

4. Who was inside the egg?

5. Who else did they meet in the land of Dinosaurs?

6. What was your favourite part?

7. There are starfish hiding throughout the book.
   How many can you find?

For the answers to this quiz and more Haggis activities,
please visit **www.laughingmonkeypublishing.co.uk**

Lightning Source UK Ltd.
Milton Keynes UK
UKHW050118130819
347819UK00002B/4/P